The Peach Tree

The Peach Tree

written by Norman Pike

illustrated by Robin & Patricia DeWitt

Inquiries should be directed to
Stemmer House Publishers, Inc.
2627 Caves Road
Owings Mills, Maryland 21117

A Barbara Holdridge book
Printed and bound in the United States
First Edition

Library of Congress Cataloging in Publication Data
Pike, Norman.
    The peach tree.

    "A Barbara Holdridge book"—Verso of t.p.
    Summary: When his peach tree is threatened by aphids,
Farmer Pomeroy brings in a horde of ladybugs to save
the tree and restore the balance of nature.
    [1. Trees—Fiction.   2. Insects—Fiction.   3. Food
chains (Ecology)—Fiction.   4. Ecology—Fiction]
I. Title.
PZ7.P6276Pe   1983   [E]   83-4393

Dedicated to my grandchildren,
Christopher, Stuart, Fritz, Ben and Patty

Everybody agreed that the new peach tree was nice:
Mrs. Pomeroy, because it might have some peaches,
her husband, who liked showing his family
how he planted fruit trees in his nursery,

the children, because it made shadow patterns with the sun,

the birds, because they could perch on its pretty branches,
and the South Wind, because it could make the leaves dance.

But one day the Aphis sisters found the peach tree.
They liked the little tree, too.

It had nice soft juicy shoots and luscious leaves.
It had tender buds of unborn peaches.

But the Aphis only wanted the sap.
And they wanted all of it.

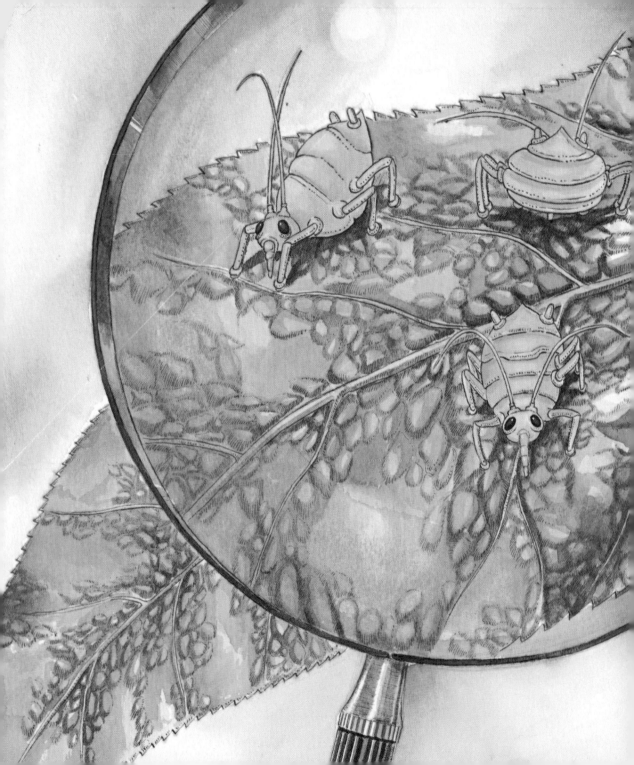

The Aphis all had hollow needle noses,
and six legs,
and big fat tummies.

And they had children,

and more children,

and the children had children,

until there was no more room on the peach tree.

They all stuck their needle noses into the soft juicy shoots,
and tasty leaves and tender buds,
and used them like soda straws,
and they drank
                    and drank
                              and drank
with their needles sunk right up to their eyes,
and their hind feet raised up in the air,
and drank until their tummies swelled.

The poor peach tree began to wilt
and its leaves lost all their shine.
The leaves no longer danced.
They just rattled.

The South Wind told the birds.
The birds must have told Mrs. Pomeroy's children,
because they ran in and told her.

And she came out and looked
and said, "What are we going to do?"
And her husband came and looked
and answered,
    "We have some friends who know what to do.
    Go tell the Ladybugs."

And the Ladybugs came
and looked the situation over.

And they knew what to do—and they did it.
They raised *their* children on the peach tree.

The Ladybugs have homely children,
who have no bright round shells
or wings
or pretty dots,
and do not look like their mammas or papas at all.

They look like little live lobsters.

They are born hungry.
And they want to grow up to be pretty like their
Moms and Dads;
They don't want to look like lobsters.
So if there are Aphis around,
They eat
        and eat
                and eat
All the Aphis they can find.
They think Aphis are delicious.

And so they ate all the Aphis on the little peach tree,
and grew into pretty, bright-colored Ladybugs.

And because the peach tree fed the Aphis,
and the Aphis fed the Ladybug children,
and the Ladybug children saved the peach tree,
and grew into pretty, bright-colored Ladybugs,
and raised *their* children on the peach tree,
it again had shiny leaves.

And the South Wind made them dance,
and the birds perched on the sturdy branches;
and it made shadow patterns with the sun,
and had the nicest, sweetest peaches
that Mrs. Pomeroy and her family ever tasted.

Colophon

Designed by Barbara Holdridge
Composed in Caslon Light and Boldface by the
    Service Composition Company, Baltimore,
    Maryland
Color separations by Capper, Inc., Knoxville,
    Tennessee
Printed by Federated Printers-Lithographers, Inc.,
    Providence, Rhode Island on 100-lb. Old Forge
    Velvetlith
Bound in Kivar Emerald Green plus Kivar Curry
    with Overprint Design 6-505 and Willow
    Green Multicolor Antique endpapers by
    Delmar Printing Company, Charlotte,
    North Carolina